THE WIZARD OF POOB

Peter Bently
Duncan Beedie

Hello! This is a story about four friendly monsters who live on Planet Pok.

This is **Nid**.

This is **Gop**.

This is **San**.

This is **Pem Pem**.

They have a funny way of talking. It's called Monsters' Nonsense.

See if you can read what they are saying. Ready?

One day the monsters were having a picnic when they heard a funny whooshing noise. It was followed by a loud CRASH!

Teg teg sprizzle phoostie nubthantle?

A strange spaceship had crash-landed nearby.

The monsters ran to help.

Plawkin quabb dax wope buddery!

Luckily, nobody was inside the crashed spaceship.
But there were lots of little bottles scattered
amongst the wreckage.

It looked just like lemonade from the Fizzy Fountain.

Before anyone could stop him, Nid opened a bottle and guzzled it down in one great gulp.

Bame vee katsdreck! Thronk whiddler bafe!

BAWP!

But it wasn't lemonade. It tasted like medicine. Nid pulled a face and let out a massive monster burp. The others laughed.

The monsters wondered where the spaceship could have come from. San found a bit of wreckage with the word POOB on it.

Chonkle wheeber nuffy, innick Poob!

POOB

Poob was a planet not far from Planet Pok.

Perhaps they should fly to Poob and see if anyone had lost a spaceship? Pem Pem and Gop agreed. But hold on – where was Nid?

Spledge doyner zark, Nid?

Thorram redyag weck yansum!

They called his name, but there was no sign of him.

They looked everywhere for Nid. He wasn't at his house.

Zepper snollbink whamp, Nid!

He wasn't at the Fizzy Fountain or at the Blue Broccoli Bush either.

Mullop chake tribbley sooch coxlaff.

It was as if he had simply vanished.

The monsters decided that he was probably having a nap somewhere. They would just have to travel to Planet Poob without him.

They clambered into Pem Pem's spaceship and took off.

Vipp vapp whoozer!

By the time the monsters landed on Planet Poob, they were feeling hungry. San hadn't eaten her picnic, so she kindly offered to share her blue broccoli sandwiches.

But she couldn't find her picnic box. She must have left it in the crashed spaceship. Bother!

Nearby there was a castle. The monsters could smell something cooking. Maybe they could get a snack there...

Prome grimpey, blart flane widdery!

The castle door was opened by a wizard. His name was Wibbwhintle and he looked worried.

Randabb plipe crove nunky dunky!

The wizard explained what had happened. A swarm of giant Space Slugs was heading for Poob, but Wibbwhintle had invented a secret magic potion to stop them.

He had loaded his spaceship with bottles of potion, then nipped back inside to get his hat.

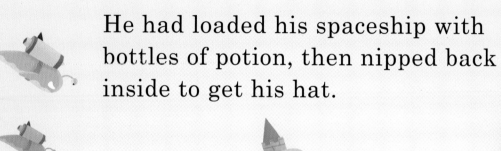

Shreeve toppit wugg wheeth faughler!

But he must have left the brake off, because when he came out again the spaceship was flying into space without him!

Wibbwhintle agreed, so they all climbed into Pem Pem's spaceship and sped off.

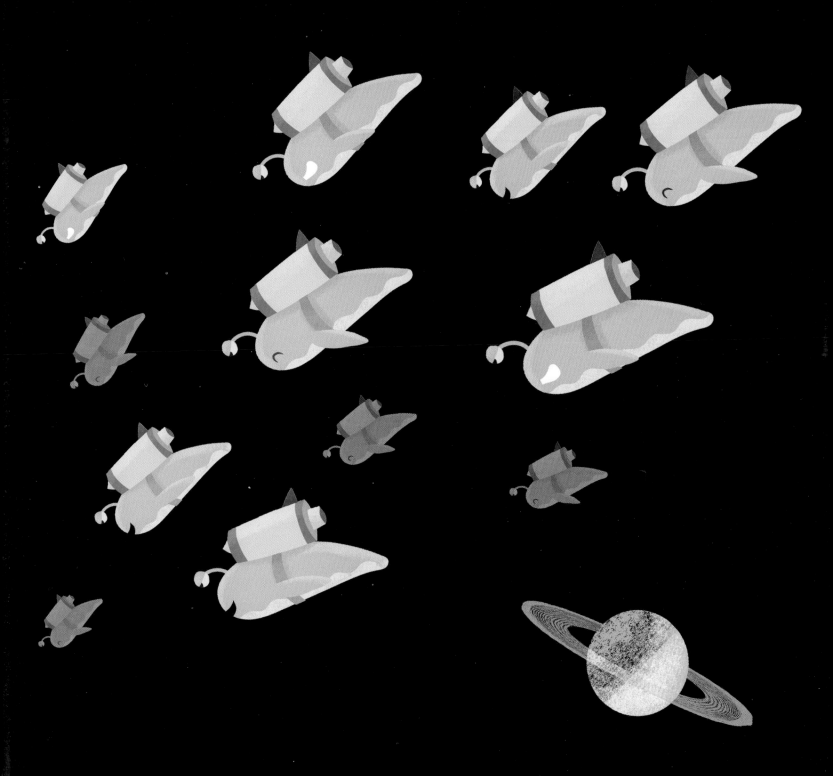

On the way back to Pok they spotted some huge green blobs. It was the giant Space Slugs on their way to Poob. There was no time to lose!

They landed near the crashed spaceship and the monsters quickly helped Wibbwhintle to gather up the bottles of potion.

Cuffaw wowker Pok jode lickerty!

They packed as many bottles as they could into Pem Pem's spaceship.

San spotted her picnic box, so she put that in the spaceship too. They would definitely need a snack after saving Planet Poob!

Crike naggler bolley chun Poob theap!

The monsters zoomed back to Poob as fast as they could.

The monsters landed on Poob and saw the swarm of Space Slugs approaching.

Blooph scride flezznogg trock jurnaff authit!

The leader of the Space Slugs was very thirsty from the long journey and demanded something to drink.

The wizard told the monsters to hand a bottle of potion to every slug.

The Space Slugs greedily guzzled down the bottles of potion. Then something strange happened.

The giant slugs all gave a great BURP – and shrank to the size of a fly!

No longer a threat, the tiny Space Slugs
flew away.

San opened her picnic box to offer everyone
a sandwich, but inside the box she found a
minute monster.

Mussion whodder
phape shapper
snollybolly kee prate!

It was Nid!

So that's where he had got to. He had drunk some potion and shrunk!

Phanch troke weast phoobin fruce!

Everyone laughed. The wizard gave Nid a new potion to make him the right size again. Then he invited all the monsters back to his castle for tea.

Reading with your monsters!

Monsters' Nonsense is all about having fun whilst learning the skills of reading. If children have fun reading, they'll want to do it more.

What helps children with their reading?

Phonics: the ability to sound out (decode) words that they don't know.

Reading comprehension: to read for meaning so that they can understand and enjoy the story.

The *Monsters' Nonsense* series is designed to support these skills to help children become successful, happy readers and to encourage a positive, shared reading experience.

The adult reader (or reading mentor) reads the main narrative – supporting reading comprehension and bringing the story alive.

The child reads the Monsters' Nonsense in the speech bubbles. These are 'non-words' to help them practise their decoding skills at a level that is right for them. It's important that your child knows that these 'non-words' are not real words and have no meaning.

More monster fun

Monster Questions Ask your child some questions about the story. For example, this is a story about four friendly monsters. How do you know they are friendly? Where in the book are there examples of them being friendly? What did they find in the wreckage of the crashed spaceship? What is the name of the wizard from Planet Poob? Why was he worried? What happened to the Space Slugs when they drank the potion? Why didn't Nid go with the others to Planet Poob?

Creative Compound Words Compound words are made when two small words are put together to form longer words, e.g. lady + bird = ladybird. The monsters use some compound words in this story, for example: scroxbott, katsdreck, redyag, randabb, flezznogg.

Firstly, identify the monsters' compound words with your child, then get some pens and strips of paper and write these words down. Use some scissors to cut each word in half. Now you can match up the pieces and put the words together yourselves to make some hilarious new compound words!

Mystery Monster Words Many of the nonsense words can be easier to read if the reader can recognise familiar sounds within the word. Get some paper and pens and pick some nonsense words. Write down part of the word, but miss out a grapheme. Give your child the page number and ask them to look for the nonsense word in the speech bubble, then say and fill in the missing grapheme. For example: p4 __ronk (th), p10 wi__ery (dd), p20 phan__ (ch). This should make the words easier to read and less of a monster mystery.

Monster Potion Make a recipe for your own potion. Think of:
• Ingredients – what do you need and how much is required?
• Method – how do you make it (e.g. stirring, baking, brewing)?
• Purpose – who is it for and what will it do?

Phonics glossary

blend to blend individual sounds together to pronounce a word, e.g. s-n-a-p blended together reads snap.

compound word a word made up of two smaller words joined together, e.g. lady + bird = ladybird.

digraph two letters representing one sound, e.g. sh, ch, th, ph.

grapheme a letter or a group of letters representing one sound, e.g. t, b, sh, ch, igh, ough (as in 'though').

High Frequency Words (HFW) are words that appear most often in printed materials. They may not be decodable using phonics (or too advanced) but they are useful to learn separately by sight to develop fluency in reading.

phoneme a single identifiable sound, e.g. the letter 't' represents just one sound and the letters 'sh' represent just one sound.

segment to split up a word into its individual phonemes in order to spell it, e.g. the word 'cat' has three phonemes: /c/, /a/, /t/.

split digraph a digraph in which the two letters making the sound are not adjacent, e.g. 'a-e' in 'cake'.

vowel digraph two vowels which together make one sound, e.g. ai, oo, ow.

It's important that your child knows the 'non-words' have no meaning. It's just Monsters' Nonsense!

Quarto is the authority on a wide range of topics.

Quarto educates, entertains and enriches the lives of our readers—enthusiasts and lovers of hands-on living.

www.quartoknows.com

Editor: Emily Pither
Designer: Verity Clark
Consultant: Carolyn Clarke

© 2018 Quarto Publishing plc

First published in 2018 by QED Publishing, an imprint of The Quarto Group.
The Old Brewery, 6 Blundell Street,
London N7 9BH, United Kingdom.
T (0)20 7700 6700 F (0)20 7700 8066
www.QuartoKnows.com

A catalogue record for this book is available from the British Library.

ISBN 978 1 78493 975 5

Manufactured in Dongguan, China TL 012018

9 8 7 6 5 4 3 2 1

MIX
Paper from responsible sources
FSC www.fsc.org FSC® C104723